Goldilocks and the Three Bears

RICHARD SCARRY'S
Easy to Read Books

Collins

Once upon a time there were three bears.
They lived happily together in
a cottage in the woods.
There was Father Bear who was a great
big bear. There was Mother Bear who
was a middle-sized bear.
And there was Baby Bear who was
a very little bear.

One sunny morning Mother Bear rose
very early and made hot porridge.
She poured some into Father Bear's
big bowl and some into her
middle-sized bowl and some into
Baby Bear's little bowl.

The porridge was very, very hot.
Father Bear said, "It's a lovely
morning. Let us go for a walk
in the woods while our porridge
cools a little.
So Father Bear, Mother Bear and
Baby Bear set off.

And as they would not be gone long,
they left the door of their cottage open.
"The breeze will help to cool
our porridge," said Mother Bear.

They had not been gone
long when a little girl
called Goldilocks
wandered by. She saw the
open door and the naughty
Goldilocks walked into
the bears' little cottage.
She saw the lovely
porridge.

She tasted the porridge
in Father Bear's big bowl.
But it was too hot.
She tasted the porridge in
Mother Bear's middle-sized bowl.
But it was too hot.
She tasted the porridge
in Baby Bear's little bowl.
It was just right.
And she ate it all up.

Then Goldilocks felt tired.
She tried Father Bear's big chair.
But it was too hard.
She tried Mother Bear's middle-sized chair.
But it was too soft.
She tried Baby Bear's little chair.
It was just right.
She sat down
and started to rock to and fro.
Suddenly "Crack!" Goldilocks
was too heavy for Baby Bear's
little chair. She landed
with a bump on the floor.

Then Goldilocks went upstairs to the
bedroom in the bears' little house.
She lay down on Father Bear's big bed.
But it was too hard.

She lay down on Mother Bear's
middle-sized bed.
But it was too soft.
She lay down on
Baby Bear's little bed.
It was just right.
And in two minutes
she was fast asleep.

In a little while a hungry Father Bear,
Mother Bear and Baby Bear came
back to their little house.
"What's this?" roared Father Bear.
"Someone's been tasting my porridge,"
when he saw a spoon in his bowl."

"Someone's been tasting *my* porridge,"
growled Mother Bear, when she saw the
spoon in her middle-sized bowl.
"And someone's been tasting *my*
porridge," squealed Baby Bear,
holding out his little bowl,
"and has eaten it all up."

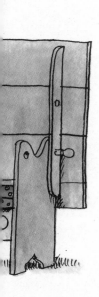

Then Father Bear looked at his big chair.
The cushion was not quite straight.
"Someone's been sitting in my chair,"
he roared.
Mother Bear looked at her middle-sized
chair. The cushions were not straight
at all.

"Someone's been sitting in *my* chair,"
she growled.
And Baby Bear looked at his little chair.
"Someone's been sitting in *my* chair," he
squealed," and has broken it all up.

"Is there a thief in our little house?"
cried the three bears. And they went
upstairs to look.
"Someone's been sleeping in my bed,"
roared Father Bear. "My covers are crumpled."
"Someone's been sleeping in *my* bed,"
growled Mother Bear. "My covers and pillow are
crumpled."

"Someone's been sleeping in *my* bed",
squealed Baby Bear. "And she's still here."

Goldilocks had not heard Father Bear roar. She had not heard Mother Bear growl. She did hear Baby Bear squeal. She woke up to see three bears. What a fright she got!

She jumped out of Baby Bear's bed.
Father Bear, Mother Bear and Baby Bear
did not move. They were too
surprised. They had never seen anyone
like Goldilocks before.

Goldilocks raced to the staircase
as quick as lightning. Down she
went and next moment was out at the open
door and running for home
faster than she had ever run before.
And Father Bear, Mother Bear and Baby
Bear never saw Goldilocks again.